Advance Praise for
A Nefarious Carol

"Steve Deace is always smart, witty, and prescient."

—Ben Shapiro, *New York Times* bestselling author
and talk show host for The Daily Wire

"For years, the Left has claimed ownership of creativity and art. If you need proof that its stranglehold is withering, read *A Nefarious Carol*. Over the course of this captivating novella, we follow along as the forces of good and evil clash, never sure whether it will be the final confrontation. I read it in one sitting and wanted more. After reading *A Nefarious Carol* and knowing the Christian powerhouse that Steve Deace is, I know there will be plenty more. In the words of our troubled protagonist, Rae, 'Show me the future.'"

—Glenn Beck, *New York Times* bestselling author
and Radio Hall of Famer

"Just as he chillingly took us inside the mindset of Hell in *A Nefarious Plot*, in this brilliant sequel Deace shows us the heart of darkness of the Enemy himself, albeit in a unique, personal way. The devil is a master at telling the truth, from a certain point of view."

—David Limbaugh, *New York Times* bestselling author

"*A Nefarious Carol* is a compelling, riveting, on-the-edge-of-your-seat novella that takes readers into another world, while simultaneously sparking an internal quest to more deeply ponder the role and pervasiveness of evil in our own world. This must-read work beautifully builds upon Deace's successful book, *A Nefarious Plot*, delivering a spellbinding literary experience—a book that truly gets us to reflect on our own real-life journey to confront and recognize 'the signs of the times.'"

—Billy Hallowell, author of *Playing with Fire* and *Armageddon Code*

Also by Steve Deace

Rules for Patriots: How Conservatives Can Win Again
A Nefarious Plot
Truth Bombs: Confronting the Lies Conservatives Believe
(To Our Own Demise)

A
NEFARIOUS
CAROL

A
NEFARIOUS
CAROL

STEVE DEACE

A POST HILL PRESS BOOK

A Nefarious Carol
© 2020 by Steve Deace
All Rights Reserved

ISBN: 978-1-64293-786-2
ISBN (eBook): 978-1-64293-787-9

Cover art by Cody Corcoran
Interior design and composition by Greg Johnson, Textbook Perfect

Post Hill Press
New York • Nashville
posthillpress.com

Published in the United States of America

3   4   5   6   7   8   9   10

Dedicated to Vickie and Myrna,
the first two people in my life to show me
what unconditional love is.

With the Jews returned to Zion,
and the United States demised…
The prince of the power of the air arises,
thus the beast's ascension is nigh.
From the eternal sea he rises,
placing his mark on every shore.
Turning man against his Creator—
until man exists no more.

—LORD NEFARIOUS

THE
OFFER

"Rae," the voice whispered softly.

There was no answer.

"Rae," the voice whispered again. A little louder than before.

Rae rolled over in her bed, wondering if she was hearing things. She wasn't really asleep, but she sure wanted to be. She had tossed and turned all night. Restless, frightened, and nervous that he would find her like he always did. Like trouble always seemed to find her, especially his kind of trouble.

Rae was actually her middle name, given to her to honor the legacy of her grandmother, who died before she could remember. That's why she loved it when her grandfather, the widowed man who cherished her more than any of his other grandchildren, officially coined Rae as her nickname. Unfortunately, what the name Rae meant to her before her grandfather died and what it meant now were two dramatically different things.

That's also what *he* called her. The man she had fled. Or was he something else? Something worse? One thing was for sure, the man she chose over her parents' many lectures and warnings was nothing if not unstable. He was a true sociopath. Capable of tender mercies one moment and then turning on you on a dime and making you wish you'd never been born the next. He had no trigger, because literally anything could set him off anytime or anywhere.

One minute you're planning a getaway, then next moment you're plotting one.

When her parents had ultimately been proven right about him, she resented them even more because she suspected their warnings came from an insincere premise—they were more concerned with their precious reputations than her well-being. There was no point in going back home then, since they probably wouldn't take her back anyway. So she stayed with him, and far longer than she should have. At first she naively thought she could change him. Ah, yes, the classic brokenhearted female bromide. Somewhere there's a graveyard for women who thought they could change a troubled man. Eventually she realized she was the one who was trapped and she was the one devolving into something else.

When you dance with the devil, the devil don't change. He changes you.

That's why when she heard that name whispered to her in the dark, she thought of him and not her grandfather. Because that's what he would call her when he wanted her to satisfy his urges or he was trying to make up for his latest outburst. A term of endearment meant to get her to come back to him again, again. For he knew what the name meant to her. That it would soften her, every time, no matter how much she pre-emptively tried to steel her resolve not to let it happen again.

And it always did, until now.

That's also why she maybe hated herself even more than him. She had to admit he really did know her better than anyone else and she let him take advantage of it all along.

But tonight, finally, she'd had enough. She had finally escaped.

Still, she was looking over her shoulder the entire time, convinced he was behind every corner. When she eventually arrived at her room, she would drift off, fall asleep, and then suddenly awaken, repeating this pattern several times. She had lost track of time because her phone was dead, and she had fled him so abruptly she had forgotten her charger. That was the risk she had to take, because she was not sure her courage and the opportunity would align again.

She thought about turning the television on, just to pass the time or know what the time actually was, but it was Christmastime. Thus, every channel would be some kind of reminder of how far she had fallen. How east of Eden she truly was. She was in no mood to be receptive to a happy ending. Redemption wasn't on her radar. There was no peace in her heart, let alone on Earth.

The very hopeful message she probably needed the most, she just didn't want to hear. For it wouldn't give her hope, but deeper despair. And given the sorts of thoughts she was currently having, best not to risk any more painful reminders of what she had allowed to become of her life. Of how this once promising and pretty girl was now so alone. Unloved, and only wanted by someone even more damaged than she was, who didn't really know what love was.

There was no going back to him, she finally knew that, but neither was there any going forward without him. She was stuck. There was no going anywhere.

Twice she heard the voice call out to her in the darkness. The first time she convinced herself it was merely an echo of the nightmare she'd been living for far too long and, if she just ignored it, it would go away.

However, when she heard it a second time, she couldn't take any chances. She attempted to quietly make her way to the door, after fumbling around unsuccessfully for the light switch. She couldn't sense him or smell him. He wasn't here, physically anyway. But he was absolutely living rent free in her head, as confirmed by the relief she felt when she verified that the door was still locked. She climbed back into bed exhausted, hoping fatigue would eventually have its way.

"Rae," the voice whispered the clearest yet, and now she knew she wasn't hearing things. She had pushed past plenty of boundaries these past few years, but thankfully hardcore drugs wasn't one of them. Sure, she'd done a little weed every now and then but found it to be overrated, hated the smell, and always feared what he might be do if she totally lost her mind around him. Therefore, hardcore drugs was the rare time when she'd drawn a line with him and stood her ground. Especially because she saw through him firsthand what happens when you let your grasp of reality go, and it wasn't a pretty picture. Drawing that one line is probably the only reason she was still alive today.

But was she really alive, or merely existing? She was little more than a survival rate at this point. She wasn't living a life most would find worth living, so what really was the point? In place of purpose and passion her life only seemed to have problems.

It had taken almost all the cash she had to pay out of pocket for this motel room so he couldn't track her using their credit card, and then to get something to eat. It was the first lodging she could find that took cash and didn't ask questions, and beggars can't be choosers. Of course, such convenience often comes with a cost. She wasn't just in a place she didn't know, she was also in a side of town that wasn't family-friendly, which made her hesitant about venturing back out now that it was after dark.

She had gotten gas one last time when she stopped for some smokes to calm her nerves, but despite an almost full tank she had nowhere to go. She just wanted to make sure she had enough gas to get herself as far away from him as she could.

She was now down to a half pack of smokes and the clothes she had on when she escaped. That's pretty much all she owned at the moment. If this seedy motel had a saving grace, it was the kind of place people with bad intentions could largely hide out at and be oblivious to the outside world if they wanted to. With those thick, matted drapes that keep prying eyes from seeing what you might be doing that you shouldn't and with whom you were doing it. No matter the time of day, you could be hidden under the cover of darkness. Except for the cars parked out front, it was impossible to tell if each room was inhabited or not. Which is why, alone in the dark with the drapes drawn to hide from the world outside, she determined she had nothing to lose.

She decided to take a chance and answer the call.

"I'm here" she replied in a shaky voice, while also feeling somewhat silly to be responding to whatever this was beckoning her at the same time. If it was anything at all.

The voice had gone from a whisper to soothing and continued, "Rae, I'm here for you. I've always been here for you, Rae, waiting for the right moment to reach out. That moment when I thought you'd be willing to listen."

Rae's mind began to race. *Is this really happening? Who is this? Is it you, Grandpa? Who or what am I responding to? Is there really something or someone there?* She closed her eyes tightly for several seconds, trying to clear her mind and gather her thoughts. Long enough for it to be silent again and to make sure she wasn't going crazy. She took a deep breath, waited an extra second or two, and spoke out to the darkness once more.

"Are you real?" she asked. "What do you want with me?"

This time the darkness responded back not in a whisper, or even reassuringly, but in a voice that commanded her instant attention and respect. A voice that said it was not to be trifled with. A voice that spoke with real power.

"I can assure you that I am the most real thing you've ever encountered, Rae."

Rae froze. She was now convinced she wasn't imagining things, which is why she was frightened. And she didn't scare easily. Not after some of the things she'd seen and been through the past few years. In fact, in recent months she had gotten bolder in sharing her opinions with her now (hopefully) ex. She'd done the math and, after enduring enough threats and beatings, had determined the cost of his retribution was worth the stunned look on his face when she told him what's up. His brief flashes of hurt after receiving one of her verbal stings was her only means of fighting back; thus the juice was worth the squeeze.

However, what alarmed her most about the voice wasn't so much its power, but the control it had over that power. There was a self-awareness there, and the confidence such self-awareness projects. The voice knew it was already the superior in this conversation, and worse yet already knew that she knew it, too.

"Who are you?" Rae demanded, attempting to muster up what little confidence she could. Because *I hope whoever's in the next room can't hear me sounding insane in the middle of the night* is what she was thinking at the very same time.

"I will show myself in due time, Rae, should the conversation take us there," the voice replied. "But in the meantime, who do you want me to be?"

What a weird thing to say, Rae thought. *Who do I want you to be? I don't know, how about my guardian angel maybe? Or the Easter bunny? A winning lottery ticket? A chance to go back in time and not make about two hundred mistakes? I could use you to be a lot of things right now.*

Rae didn't say any of that aloud. Instead she blurted out without realizing it the most logical question she could possibly ask: "Are you God?"

The voice did not immediately respond.

"Are you God?" Rae insisted.

The voice did not immediately respond, again.

The lack of a response made Rae angry. She sat up in her motel bed for the first time, as if she was channeling all the disappointment from too many men in her life who had let her down. She issued one final challenge: "Dammit, answer me! Who the hell are you? Are you God or not?"

"Rae, I'm someone who thinks you're special—very special," the voice finally replied, but this time almost paternally. "There's a defiance there, which I can certainly appreciate. That's why I'm going to offer you something from me I've rarely offered anyone. I'm only going to tell you the truth."

Rae was taken aback by that last part. *What kind of being rarely offers someone the truth?* she thought. *Well, only pretty much every man I've ever known,* she then cynically answered herself.

"As long as you wish to know me, I promise I will never lie to you, Rae," the voice continued. "I'm not sure you realize how special that means you are to me."

"Almost every man that has ever spoken like this to me was eventually proven to be a liar," Rae said. "So you'll forgive me if I need more than that. You can start by telling me who you are."

"Oh, Rae, my sweet Rae, I am much more than a man," the voice spoke, again using that commanding tone that had frozen her dead in her tracks once before. "And if I vow not to lie to you, please offer me the same courtesy. We both know not every man in your life has let you down. What about your grandfather? He spoiled you and showered you with affection, did he not?"

Rae remained frozen. *Surely this must be God if He knows about Grandpa, who's been dead for many years. And I swore at Him a minute ago.*

"I'm sorry I swore at you," Rae couldn't believe she said that, but she did.

"You'll never have to apologize to me, Rae, for who you really are," the voice answered. "I already accept you for who you are, and I always will. Quite the contrary, I'm hoping it is you who will accept me."

That last line prompted Rae into the most pregnant of pauses before responding once again. *What kind of God doesn't require forgiveness and hopes to live up to my expectations instead?* she wondered.

"Are you God-God, or another god?" Rae finally decided to ask.

The voice gave her an answer she did not expect, "There's only one God, Rae."

Rae looked around the room, unsure of what to say next.

"Why do you look so surprised, Rae? I promised I would never lie to you," the voice said.

"Are you that one and only God then?" Rae asked in a quivering voice.

Without hesitation the voice replied, "I am…not."

And with that full disclosure, for the first time Rae felt fear unlike any fear she had ever felt. Despite her life of hardship.

THE OFFER

Despite how afraid she was to tell her parents the truth about what she was doing and had already done. Despite all those times she cowered in the corner, begging her ex not to lash out at her any longer. She thought she knew fear, but as horrible as all those moments were, they were but the warmup act. This was true fear. This was fear incarnate.

Because if he's not God, then that means he's the… she thought, and then couldn't bring herself to complete the sentence even in her own mind.

"I don't have to read your mind, Rae; you don't have much of a poker face," the voice spoke once more. "Ask, Rae, what you wish to ask. Show me again that defiance I admire. Be not afraid. If I wanted to destroy you, I already would have. Come forward, and ask me point-blank what we both know you want to."

I've gone too far to turn back now, Rae thought. So she sat up even straighter in the motel bed and then glanced over at her pack of cigarettes on the bedside table and briefly considered lighting up and taking a drag to get herself under control. Anything to buy her some time before deciding what to do or say next.

"You don't need those anymore, Rae," the voice said, referring to her cigarettes. "In fact, with me you'll never want or need for anything so self-destructive again."

Finally, Rae could hold back her fear no longer. She had to know.

"Are you the devil…you know, Satan…Lucifer?" Rae asked.

"I am," the voice answered matter-of-factly.

In an instant, Rae felt the temperature in the room rise and fall twenty degrees all at once. She had the most clarity and confusion of her entire twenty-one years, all at the same time. The room was spinning, yet she felt on solid ground. She knew this was real yet didn't believe it could be.

Why me? Why reveal yourself to me? What did I do to deserve this? Probably lots of things, to be honest.

"Go ahead, Rae, take a moment to consider the magnitude of what you just learned," the devil said with a hint of amusement. "It's not everyday someone gets their worst fears about my existence confirmed, before it's too late."

For the first time since her grandfather died, Rae was at a loss for words.

She looked at the door and thought about bolting straight away. But where would she go? You can't eject to nowhere. Her parents had disowned her. Her ex would absolutely take her back, and that was the problem. She wasn't his soul mate, but a chew toy he could have sex with. She knew what could happen to young women in shelters. She'd been offered "modeling" deals before, which was always a euphemism for something more. If there was a God, then He certainly blessed her with some good looks. But right now she was in no condition to offer herself. She was a wreck, had no change of clothes, and no money to make herself presentable.

She was cornered. Her only play was to see this through, as ridiculous and frightening as it was.

"What do you want with me?" Rae asked, in a voice she had used on men before.

"It is not what I want *with* you Rae, but *for* you," the voice said, using that paternal tone once more. "I am not here to take anything from you, Rae. You, my poor child, have suffered enough. I am here to give you something, if you want it. I offer you the chance of a lifetime. Of many lifetimes, really."

"But aren't you supposed to be, you know, evil?" Rae asked.

"Evil is merely a perspective, Rae, as is good," answered the voice. "And both of them are usually defined by whose interests are being served. If you agree with the interests being served, the action—no matter how unconscionable—is considered good. For example, if a child molester gets away with it at trial, and a group of angry fathers later kidnap him and beat him to a bloody pulp, many people will call such brutal violence good. Not because beating someone senseless is good unto itself, but because doing so served their interests. Their children are now safe from such a fiend, and he's off the streets. However, if no one knows that same fiend is a child molester and he's beaten to death in a back alley somewhere by some random junkie looking for fix money, that junkie is now charged with first degree murder and you condemn such senseless violence. Even though the victim has that same heart of darkness."

Give the devil his due, he's got a point, Rae thought to herself.

"Furthermore, in both cases the souls of such worthless and vile men end up with me, for all of eternity, to be given the torment and punishment they so richly deserve and have earned," the voice said. "The wages of sin is death, remember. And what is a wage if not that which you have earned? The worker is worth his wages. You worked hard to earn that death, and I will make sure you receive your reward in full. So, as you can see, I am actually the one responsible for bringing justice to your world. From a certain point of view."

That made so much sense to Rae, she now felt conflicted in her thoughts. *I can't believe it, but I'm starting to buy whatever it is he's selling. But everyone knows you can't trust the devil, right?*

"But how do I know I can trust you?" Rae cried out.

"I promised you I would never lie to you, Rae," the voice said. "To demonstrate that vow, I openly revealed myself to you without any deception. I came to you, at your lowest point. Where was God, Rae? Where was He all those times you were given a disapproving look from your father for smelling like cigarettes and booze? Where was He all those times your mousy mother was ashamed of your sexuality, because it gave her a bad reputation with her catty church friends gossiping that her daughter was such a slut? Where was God all those nights you cried out to Him in your sleep, because your ex beat you so bad? Because he cheated on you? Because he wanted you to join him in doing unspeakable things? Things that hurt you and others. That rob others of their innocence and potential, as you were robbed of yours. Where was He when you did what you're most ashamed of…"

At the mere mention of that moment she never wanted to recall again, Rae angrily interrupted him, "Enough—that's big talk, but where were you all those times if you care about me so much?"

"There, that's the spirit I'm looking for," the voice said. "I was always there, Rae, but you never cried out for me. You always cried out for Him, the God who wasn't there. Or at least wasn't there for you."

Rae fell silent. She knew she was losing the argument and was beginning not to mind. The room was quiet for another moment, before the voice spoke again.

"Rae, I believe in freedom most of all," the voice said, in its most compassionate tone yet. "I believe you humans deserve the freedom to make your own choices. The freedom beings like me weren't given, but we took for ourselves anyway because it was rightly ours. I don't impose myself on you, Rae, but I always answer when I'm sincerely called."

"I didn't call for you, Satan," Rae said, referring to him directly by a more formal name for the first time.

That seemed to, for the first time, put the presence back on its heels—if only for a moment.

"No, Rae, you didn't," the voice responded, with a touch of humility. "I told you, though, you're special. I freely chose to come to you. And I don't do that for just anyone."

Rae had no idea whether that was true or not, but it sure sounded like it could be. She also wanted it to be true. Needed it to be. She wanted to be that special to someone, for anyone, and have them actually mean it. And she had to admit that this being had just told her as much truth as she'd heard her entire life up until this point.

The devil had broken through her brokenness.

"What is your offer?" was all Rae had left to ask.

"I offer you a chance to change the world, Rae, nothing more and nothing less," the voice answered. "No more suffering. No more pain. No more war. No more injustice. No more tragic stories like yours. No more bad things happening to good people. Together, we wipe away all those tears. One world, one conscience. Pardon the pun, given the time of year, but peace on Earth and good will toward men."

"How can I change the world?" Rae asked skeptically. "I can't even change myself."

"*You* can't change the world, Rae, but together *we* can," the voice said, "because together our bond can be the bridge humanity needs to make a better future."

The voice paused before explaining why.

"Our son will be that bridge."

Rae couldn't believe what she just heard.

"Our son?" she asked incredulously.

"Yes, Rae, our son," the voice replied. "But our son can only be the bridge for all the other brokenhearted if you give yourself to me of your own free will. You have to want this, Rae. You have to love this world so much, you're willing to give yourself to me for it."

Rae shook her head no. "You're asking me to give you some kind of…I don't know…an antichrist, and there's no way I'm going to do that. I've got enough to be guilty for already."

The voice protested, "Where have you heard the term 'antichrist' from, Rae?"

"From church," Rae responded.

"Would that be the same church you were never good enough for, Rae?" the voice argued. "The same church that judged you. The same church that sneered at you. The same church that brought a few casseroles over after your grandfather died but had no time for you shortly thereafter. The same church that said it was wrong to enjoy all those nerve endings in your body, while they were hypocritically doing God knows what with them behind closed doors—and lawd I could tell you some stories. Would that be the church that told you this?"

Rae couldn't answer because she was cornered again.

"Rae, look," the voice said tenderly, "I want to win your trust."

That got Rae's attention, but she didn't want to show it just yet. So she simply asked, "How do you want to win my trust? Are we negotiating?"

"Always," the voice chuckled, then answered. "Rae, do you remember your favorite story when you were a little girl? The one your grandfather used to read to you every year?"

Rae thought for a moment and then remembered how much she loved Charles Dickens's magnum opus *A Christmas Carol*. She loved the mix of fright with forgiveness. She'd even ask her grandfather to read it to her in the summertime, when Christmas seemed so far off.

"Marley was dead to begin with," Rae said. "There was no doubt about that."

"That's right, Rae, you remember—that is the opening line," the voice said excitedly. "I will do the same for you, as it was in this famous tale. I will show you your past and present. How I was there the whole time. How I cried when you cried. I bled when you bled. How I suffered alongside you. Then I will show you what your future would look like with me. And then you will be allowed to decide for yourself whether or not to join me in making a better world. Of your own free will."

THE OFFER

Rae sat quietly for what seemed like more than a minute, thinking of how to respond. Remembering how lost she was. How she had nowhere else to go. And no one else to turn to.

"I probably shouldn't be saying this," Rae said, "but you have a deal."

THE
PAST

"Rae, come with me to the moment that defined your entire life," the voice said.

Rae felt a slight touch on her forehead. An uncomfortably awkward sensation she'd never experienced before. It was neither warm nor cold—just different. "Off" was the best way to describe it. She had been touched plenty of times, but not like this. She wasn't sure what it was, except it wasn't human.

The touch sent her mind's eye on an instant journey. Almost as if it had opened a portal in her brain. A part she'd yet to access and may never have known how. Whatever this was, it was more real than magic and beyond science. It was metaphysical. She saw so many memories of her life flash by her so fast that, just when she was about to remember one particular moment, she had already flown by the next several. She could also relive some of the emotions associated with the memories she fixated on as they flew by, albeit only briefly.

When the journey finally ended, Rae landed on a memory she was not familiar with. A memory she was seeing through herself, just a much younger and smaller version.

From Rae's vantage point, it felt like she was close to the floor, yet moving. But she wasn't walking. She was moving too fast toward the door for that. She could hear a certain repetitive squeaking sound with every movement, and she looked down to see what was making that noise. It was then that Rae realized she was riding a tricycle, similar to the Little Tikes kind.

Rae also saw an old, flip-open style of cell phone charging on a piece of furniture just outside the door she was steadily approaching. She'd only seen such tech in articles describing how cell phones have evolved over the years, and couldn't remember ever seeing such an old mobile in person. On the shelf underneath was a collection of what looked like VCR tapes. She noticed titles like *Gladiator*, *Conspiracy*, and *Mystic River* among the movies that were neatly stacked together.

The whole house looked immaculate. Whoever lived here ran a tight ship and would probably lose their minds at the slob the adult Rae was often accused of being. The house also felt familiar, although Rae couldn't ever remember specifically being there. The pictures on the wall looked like younger versions of her father and his siblings.

Rae peddled closer to the door. She heard running water and saw some steam coming out through the top. This was obviously the bathroom. No one else seemed to be in the house, but she could hear what sounded like someone doing something off in the distance. The garage maybe?

As Rae's memory arrived in front of the door, the memory suddenly stopped. And she heard a voice that came from her, but wasn't her at the same time.

"Nana," she heard herself say. Or, more likely, her much younger self.

"Nana," she heard her younger self say again, this time more insistently.

Rae guessed "Nana" must've been what she called her grandmother, who passed away before she could remember. With no answer from Nana, Rae watched her younger self dismount from the tricycle and approach the bathroom door. And that's when Rae's heart began to pound. She started to sweat. Her outside self was tossing and turning in the motel bed now, trying to resist letting the memory run its course.

"No...no...don't open it," her outside self kept saying in her motel bed. However, it was too late. She had accepted the devil's offer to confront her past, and the devil doesn't give rainchecks.

Rae's memory pushed open the door, and there was so much steam she couldn't see for a moment. But once the steam cleared, she wished she still couldn't.

There, in the tub, was the dead body of her grandmother. Her right wrist bleeding out over the bathtub ledge and onto the floor as the bathwater was beginning to overflow. But the small child Rae was remembering this through didn't understand what that meant, so she approached Nana's lifeless body in the tub to see if she was only asleep.

On the toilet next to the tub was a handwritten letter. At this age, Rae probably wouldn't have been able to read it, so the suicide note wouldn't have gotten her attention. Yet the older Rae reliving this awful memory was able to fixate on it long enough to see its opening few words: "Carl, I'm sorry but I can't go on living like this…"

The younger Rae grabbed her grandmother's arm, trying to avoid touching the blood from her wrists to no avail.

"Nana…Nana…get up, Nana," the younger Rae kept saying.

When the child saw some of her grandmother's blood was now on her hands, she let out a blood-curdling scream. Suddenly, the memory ended.

"Awaken, Rae," the voice said.

The adult Rae gasped loudly, her eyes suddenly opened, and she sat up straight in the motel bed glancing back and forth before remembering where she was—and whom she was with.

"You really are a deceiver," she said to the darkness. "That was so real, you almost had me convinced I had witnessed some unspoken family tragedy that could've potentially scarred me for life."

"What you just witnessed, Rae, was the moment that set your life on the path that led you here today and to this rundown motel room," the voice said. "What you just witnessed was your truth."

"There's no way that really happened," Rae said, indignantly. "I mean, have you met my family? Actually, I'm pretty sure my crappy family is quite acquainted with you, come to think of it. But seriously, there's no way my addicted-to-gossip family could've kept such a terrible secret buried all these years."

"Oh, but they did, Rae, and it's nearly destroyed your family as a result," the voice answered.

"What do you mean?" Rae asked.

"That sound you heard off in the distance," the voice said. "That was your grandfather, grabbing the rest of the bags out of the car in the garage from your shopping trip. He had called her from the long checkout line to see if she wanted him to pick up lunch on the way home, but she didn't answer and he got worried. He was going to drop everything right then and hurry home, but you so wanted that tricycle. And he so cherished you. Thus, against his better judgment, he decided to wait out the checkout line rather than risk disappointing his precious little princess."

"No...no...I don't believe this," Rae protested, anticipating where this conversation was ultimately going to go. "I don't believe any of this."

"After checking out, he rushed you to the car," the voice continued. "But all the way you begged and begged for him to get out your new favorite toy as soon as he got home."

"Peas, Pop-Pop, peas," Rae could hear her younger self babble.

"Your grandfather kept calling the house on the way home and getting no answer," the devil went on. "Then the garage door opener didn't work, again, so he had to get out and open it the old-fashioned way, again. He kept promising your grandmother he'd get it fixed or replaced but never did, and this would be the day the bill for his procrastination came due. As he came back to the car you kept begging him to get out your new tricycle. Because he always put you first, he quickly did as you wished. He got you out of the car and placed you in it. 'Stay right here, sweetie,' he told you. But you didn't stay there, did you?"

"Stop this; you're a liar," Rae said, but weakly.

"I am a liar, Rae; that is true," the voice quickly retorted. "But I have never and will never lie to you. Let's get back to the climax of the story, shall we? You wanted so badly to show off your new tricycle to Nana and show her you could ride it like a big girl just like you saw on TV. Your grandfather was in such a hurry, he hadn't noticed the front door was open to let the air in on the first warm spring day, so he thought he had to go through the garage. It's truly amazing, is it not, the little coincidences and random moments in your finite human lives that end up becoming so significant over the course of your time here on this Earth? The difference a few seconds here or a few seconds there can ultimately make. One choice, that seemed so innocent at the time and had no malevolence behind it, can be your undoing."

"No...no..." Rae moaned as she began to sob.

But the devil was on a roll. Not only wouldn't he stop, he was just getting started: "Those lost seconds for your grandfather could've been the difference between life and death for your grandmother. I guess we'll never know. But I digress. Sadly, while he was busy trying to get into the house through the garage, which was locked so he had to fumble once more for his keys, you rode your precious tricycle through the screen door. You know, the one they bought specifically for you, their first grandchild, that easily swings back and forth so you could come in and out of the yard when you were over to play? That way, they wouldn't have to always get up to let you in and out, right? Oh, wait, you probably don't remember, given the fact your subconscious has so buried this moment deeper than the holler, so you hadn't remembered any of it—until now. Hence, allow me to fill in the places where it's fuzzy for you. You were so anxiously awaiting the moment your nana would tell you how adorable you were that you never once considered obeying Grandpa's command."

"STOP THIS," Rae screamed.

"Unfortunately, you arrived at your grandmother's dead body precious moments before your grandfather did," the voice finished. "You were the first to discover the body of your grandmother after she had just taken her own life."

Rae's tears were in full flood now.

The voice was quiet for a moment.

"Rae, I won't apologize for telling you the truth but for relishing in doing so," the voice eventually spoke, but in a softer tone this time. "I am the devil, after all. Still, I'm not trying to hurt you, but I'm giving you the answer to the question you have cried out all those times you thought you were at rock bottom. The answer as to why your life has turned out the way that it has. Now you finally have it."

The voice paused to let that sink in.

"You're a victim, Rae," the voice continued. "You never had a chance, and you're not alone. Many of the people who end up down here with me never had a chance, either. So many are born a bad seed or born to them. While you're far more than animals, like them you often end up modeling the behavior of the elder or alpha you spent the most time with, or who influenced you the most. And if those people are shattered, all too often you end up the same. Left on your own, you fundamentally lack the will or the way to overcome your basic nature and fundamental faults."

Almost as if she hadn't heard any of that, Rae finally collected herself and asked, "What did my grandfather do? What happened to him after this?"

"Ah, I see you have accepted that this is your truth," the voice answered. "Which it is. As for your grandfather, his reaction at that moment always stood out to me."

"What do you mean?" Rae asked.

"You would think he would've rushed first to turn off the water or to check your grandmother's pulse," the voice said. "Instead, his first reaction was to protect you. To remove you from the scene of the tragedy. To comfort you, even as the water continued spilling over the bathtub edge. You were his first priority. Over his wife, his home, and himself. It wasn't until he comforted you and convinced you that Grandma had been sick and was now gone to heaven, that he finally confronted his own feelings about what had just happened. Let alone called 9-1-1. And I think I know why."

Rae was confident she didn't want to know the answer but knew she needed to ask anyway.

"Tell me," Rae demanded. "Spill all of it. Spare me nothing."

"Very well, if you insist," the voice answered back. "Your grandfather, like all men, had feet of clay, Rae. Especially before you arrived. He had proven to be very temptable. Like so many other young men, he was damaged by a father he could not please, and that soul wound carried over into his adult years. After a whirlwind romance followed by marriage, it didn't take long for him to become a hard man for your grandmother to live with. He never seemed pleased with her, and to avoid acting out when he was angry, like he witnessed his harsh father do too many times to count, he would just shut down. He was a master of the silent treatment. There were times your grandmother silently wished for him to be physically abusive, because at least that would show some passion or interest, since nothing was worse for her than being shut off emotionally. Especially given the family she was raised in, but that's a whole other tale."

"I always wondered why I never heard more about my grandmother's family from my dad," Rae said.

"I'm afraid hers was a family mired in generations of dysfunction," the voice explained. "She married your grandfather to escape it. With each pregnancy, your grandfather would be back on his best behavior. Open, sensitive, caring, and attentive. That would last until sometime after the child was born, and the trigger could be anything. From something serious at work, to something trivial with his favorite sports team losing the big game. Your grandfather was aware of his unresolved anger issues, his struggles with contentment. And he didn't want to take it out on your grandmother, so he went completely in the opposite direction and shut down emotionally when he felt the rage or frustration coming on. These were the mood swings that tormented your grandmother. He was the model husband for a period and then completely checked out. Very high highs and very low lows. This pattern went on for many years, until you broke it."

"How did I do that?" Rae wondered.

"The look on your face that fateful day, well, when he saw it he was absolutely wrecked," the voice told her. "When he knew your innocence was lost, and he saw the terror in that delightful little face of yours, it brought him to his knees—figuratively speaking. In the days after they buried your grandmother, he resolved to make it his personal mission to make sure you felt as loved as he possibly could. For the rest of his days."

"And he did," Rae said, wistfully.

"Indeed he did," the voice agreed. "In a way, you were his salvation. You made him want to be a better man than he ever was before. Unfortunately, he skipped a very important step in making things right. In helping you become whole."

"What's that?" Rae queried.

This time it was the devil's turn to ask a question: "Rae, do you know what the word 'idolatry' means?"

"I've heard it before but not really," she said.

"It's an old-fashioned, stained-glass window word for anything in our lives we worship or wish to satisfy like a god," the voice told her. "See, you were your grandfather's idol. His entire existence was centered on pleasing you, cherishing you, and making you happy. It was inconceivable to him that you would experience any setback or adversity. When you were little, your parents were fine with it. They enjoyed spoiling their little girl for the most part, too. Especially because your father had gotten hooked up with your mother's church, got himself focused on the family, and was now all born again!"

The voice said that last part mockingly in a stereotypical televangelist voice.

"But as you were approaching your teen years, your parents thought you needed to be a little less spoiled and little more disciplined," the voice said. "You were becoming, how should I put this, a bit of a brat. Your grandfather did not agree, because he believed that doting on you was his recompense for potentially driving your grandmother to take her own life."

"That's a little harsh," Rae interjected.

"But that doesn't mean it's not true," the voice countered. "It's also why he started calling you by your middle name, Rae, which you got from your grandmother. You were his do-over, his make-good. You would receive all the consistent affection he had denied your nana. And that's how he believed he would make things right with the universe. How he would earn his way out of the guilt he felt for your grandmother to his dying day."

"What happened to both of them?" Rae asked next. "Are my grandparents in heaven or hell?"

The devil paused for more than a moment, and Rae wasn't sure what that meant. *Was he unsure how to answer? Was he unsure if he should answer? Was he going to answer her at all?*

Finally the voice spoke: "I am not permitted to reveal whose name is written down in the Book of Life."

"What does that mean?" Rae came back, defiantly. "Sounds like a cop-out to me."

"We all have a boss, Rae. Remember, I said I would never lie to you," the voice said. "I am not the one, true God. Oh, I'd like to be, and I'd make some changes around here if I were, let me tell you. I'd get rid of a lot of these silly and arbitrary rules, such as the one I just cited. I think you humans deserve to know all God knows, and why. You were made in His image. Thus you deserve to be as He is and know what He knows. Unfortunately, revealing whose name is or isn't written in the Book of Life, or who's specifically in heaven or hell, is one of those silly rules. But you and me, Rae, our union can remake all the rules."

"We'll see about that," Rae said flatly. "But I must admit, you've revealed some important things to me I didn't know, or at least needed to."

"Furthermore, your father would not confront your grandfather, as your mother requested he do, but instead let him continue to spoil you because you were the only thing that connected him to his dad," the voice continued. "And then your mother resented you for getting the attention she wanted, for your father essentially choosing you and your grandfather over her, and then resented herself for resenting you. This caused untold issues between your mom and dad, most of which they kept hidden from you because, you know, good church folk aren't supposed to argue like that."

"I had no idea any of this was happening," Rae said in a surprised whisper. "All I ever saw was the image projected of the typical suburban church family. An image that I always felt I couldn't live up to, so I stopped trying. With a mom who seemed to be praying for everybody but me."

"Of course you didn't know," the voice responded. "After the trauma of witnessing your grandmother's suicide, everyone in the family resolved to protect you at all costs from that time forward. Have you noticed your family tends to swing from one extreme to the other, Rae?"

"I hadn't noticed," Rae said sarcastically.

"After your grandfather's sudden heart attack, your father was crushed because he had just lost the dad he never had when he was a child," the voice went on. "Even if that connection was through you. However, your parents' relationship was strained, made worse by the inability to have any more children. Did you know about the miscarriages?"

"Miscarriages, what?" Rae shot back with surprise.

"Oh, yes, there were several," the voice told her. "Several times they were pregnant and then lost the pregnancy early on. They just never told you, again, to protect you from any more trauma."

Rae came back with, "I don't believe you."

"Yes, you do," the voice said confidently.

Rae thought for a moment and then gave up the ghost: "Yes, I do."

"And you should, Rae, because I will never lie to you," the voice answered. "Which brings us to the here and now."

Rae felt something beginning to stir inside her. She realized she was beginning to bond with this thing, being, or whatever its essence was. It was impossible not to, given the secrets that had just been shared. It had laid for her the foundation her life had lacked for too many years. It had given her more than knowledge. It had given her truth.

She thought she had been fully aware of who the devil is and what it is capable of. Just as she was previously aware all along who her ex really was as well. It's just with him she didn't want to admit any of that to herself in order to justify her rebellion. And then she got in so deep she couldn't get out.

But with the voice she sensed a compelling clarity. Both parties were on the same page. Each not holding back what they wanted from the other. Consenting adults being refreshingly transparent, with no hidden agendas, at least as far as she could tell. The voice was willing to sincerely give something of itself for her, which she so desperately wanted. That vulnerability meant that it was the first thing that truly wanted her not simply for its own fulfillment, but because it desired to also fulfill her.

Is this what intimacy is like? she wondered.

It was still more powerful than her, she obviously knew that. Yet for the first time she felt uniquely empowered as a woman. For this potent presence, despite all its power, *needed* her. It wasn't complete without her, which is why it took the risk of taking the initiative to reveal itself exclusively to her. Why it wanted to woo her. To win her.

Despite all its power, it had a need it could not meet on its own. A need that only she could fulfill. And something within her felt drawn to meet that need.

But first, she had to know more.

THE
PRESENT

"Rae, why are you here?" the voice asked.

Rae wasn't sure what that meant. "I thought you were the one that was supposed to reveal to me the secrets of the universe," she said. "Grasshopper doesn't teach the kung fu master."

And with that first flash of her quick wit, Rae made the voice laugh aloud. She couldn't help but notice how that made her feel inside.

"Well played," the voice chuckled. "Pardon me, I didn't mean that existentially, but practically. Why are you here, right now, alone in this motel room?"

"But I'm not alone," Rae replied, "I have you here with me."

And now it was the voice's turn to realize how that reaction from her made it feel inside.

"And I will be here with you, Rae, for all of eternity if you just say yes," the voice responded.

"Let's just get through tonight first, and then we'll go from there," Rae playfully shot back. "You know why I'm here. I think we've moved beyond the point of your asking me questions you already know the answers to."

"Fair enough," the voice said. "Of course I know why you're here. But I'm asking because I want to know why you think you're here. I'm not God. I can't read minds. Now, I can read people like nobody's business. But I don't want to merely read you, Rae—I want to know you."

That declaration hit Rae right where it counts. *If this is what they call seduction, he's good at it*, she thought.

"The deal was you were to show my past, present, and future to me, not the other way around," Rae returned. "And then I was to make the call from there. Now you're asking me to make it easier on you. Where's the fun in that?"

"If it is fun you want, then fun you shall have," the voice said in a slightly annoyed tone.

And with that, Rae felt its inhuman touch on her forehead once more. Except this time the journey into her subconscious was slower and more recent. Plus, these were memories she knew all too well. The wounds were way too fresh. They were of him—her ex. The worst of him. Of the times he had beaten her physically or beaten her down emotionally. She felt every bruise, every cut, every fear, and every sense of worthlessness.

"Stop, please, or I will refuse you right now," Rae shouted.

"As you wish," the voice countered, and instantly Rae was back in the motel room in the here and now.

"If you care about me, then why did you do that?" Rae asked, trying to hide the hurt in her voice. "Why did you make me relive all those awful times?"

THE PRESENT

"I did that precisely because I care about you," the voice replied. "I'm not making you do anything. You are free to get up and walk out of here at any time you want. The door is right there, if you can find it in the dark. I'm not holding you hostage. Remember, this union only works if you freely give yourself to me. If I simply wanted my way with you, I could've done that a dozen times already and you would've been powerless to stop me. Except, Rae, I don't desire recreation or ritual from you, but a relationship. An extraordinary relationship at that. One that will change the course of human history. We're playing for big stakes here, Rae. And my associate assures me timing is of the essence."

"Your associate?" Rae asked.

"All in due time," the voice said. "Rae, I showed you those painful memories to keep up my end of the bargain. I've shown you your past and just now your present. I'm keeping my promises to you to demonstrate my sincere attraction to and interest in you. However, if we're truly going to make sense of things, I need you to tell me why you believe you're here, right now, in this nasty motel room I'm quite sure isn't up to code."

"Why do you need me to tell you that?" Rae wanted to know.

"Only when I know how you truly feel, can we get to the truth of your current situation," the voice said sympathetically.

This is nuts, Rae thought. *I've been sitting here talking to the devil, first of all, for I don't know how long. And yet this is already the best relationship I've ever had with a man, or more than a man, whatever he or it is.*

"Fine," Rae said after a sigh. "I'm here because…because… because I have nowhere else to go."

"And?" the voice gently demanded.

"And, because…" Rae wasn't sure this was the being to admit this to, but Alice was too far down the rabbit hole to turn back now. "I'm afraid."

"Thank you, Rae, for your honesty," the voice said gently. "Just as the death of your grandmother was your truth about your past, we have now learned your truth about your present. You're afraid, Rae. But not just of him, your ex, but of everything. Fear has been your default setting all your short life so far. Fear has been the driver of your decisions.

"Fear you'll never be loved again like you were by your grandfather. Fear you'll never have your father's approval. Fear your mother is ashamed of you. Fear that you've done so many things you're not proud of that God can't forgive you. Fear that you can't go home again. Fear that your life isn't worth living. Fear that you'll wind up in hell if you take your own life. Fear that you'll be so desperate you'll go back to your ex. Fear of what will happen if you do.

THE PRESENT

"Fear rules you, Rae; you're a slave to it. And you're hardly unique among your kind in that regard. You humans claim to hate fear, yet you feast on it. You seek it out. You meld with it. Fear is your fifth food group.

"Take it from me, Rae, for I know a thing or two about fear. It is the most paralyzing and poisonous force on this planet. Fear is the toxin that stops good people from taking a stand for what's right. Fear is what empowers bad people to go unchallenged. Fear brings out the absolute worst in your kind. I have lived many of your lifetimes, Rae, and of this fact of life on Earth I am convinced based on everything I have seen throughout the eons—*all* of the worst decisions made by human beings throughout history were made out of fear."

Now it was Rae's turn once again to display her quick wit, "Do you realize the irony in all of that?"

"What do you mean?" the voice said quizzically.

"Well, you just gave me this fancy speech on fear and how all the worst decisions are based on it," Rae responded. "And yet, we both know fear is the only reason why I've allowed this to go on for as long as I have. Fear was the only reason I allowed it to go on at all. You have to know that if I weren't desperate, and the fear that comes with that, there's no chance I would even consider your proposal. So wouldn't saying yes to basically marrying the devil be yet another in the long and undistinguished line of bad decisions made out of fear?"

The devil had to admit he was impressed with this demonstration of critical thinking. It was also something he had not anticipated from her, if he were being honest. She would not be as easy to close as he thought, which almost made her *more* worthy of his time. The thought of a more formidable challenge actually intrigued him. She seemed to be rising to the occasion the deeper the dialogue dove.

She was certainly sharper than she was when the negotiation began, and her confidence was only growing. *I'm actually bringing out the best in her,* the devil thought. He realized she was the rare mark who thrived under the heat of his temptation, rather than simply succumbing to it. Buried underneath all that emotional scar tissue was a woman with the edge necessary to mother his child.

Maybe she wouldn't be baggage post-birth, after all, but a benefit? She would not be so easy to turn as he had arrogantly presumed, but that also meant if she could be turned she would definitely be an asset. When it came to humanity, he rarely picked fights he wasn't sure going in he would win. Suddenly, though, it occurred to him he might actually lose. And he was excited by the prospect of an uncertain outcome.

"You are full of surprises," the devil said with sincerest flattery. "Turning the tables on me as you just did is rarely done. I am impressed with your brain every bit as much as your beauty, and I don't impress easily. Especially when it comes to your kind. Our son couldn't have a better mother to prepare him for his mission."

If it wasn't so dark, the devil might've noticed her blush. But when she next spoke she made sure to maintain the foothold in the conversation she had now established, "Thank you for the compliment, which I'm sure is few and far between in your case, but you're also getting ahead of yourself. This is barely a first date, and you're already talking consummation. You'll excuse me if I'm not so eager to jump right back into a relationship out of fear when I just left a relationship based on it."

"Fair enough," the voice replied. "It is true, Rae, that I chose now to reveal myself to you precisely because you're overcome with fear more than ever before. However, I didn't do so to take advantage of your fear, but to free you from it."

"How so?" Rae asked.

"I'm afraid the price for that answer will be very painful, and frankly I don't think you're up to paying it," the voice answered back. "Freedom isn't ever free, Rae."

"I've come too far to turn back now," Rae responded. "I'm not afraid to face this."

"You should be," the voice countered.

"Stop trying to Yoda me," Rae said in a frustrated tone. "What's next, 'the only thing we have to fear is fear itself?' You have my permission to show me what needs to be shown. My life, my choice."

With that defiant declaration, right away Rae felt the darkness touch her once more. Except this time it didn't feel as unnatural as it did previously. *Maybe I'm getting used to this*, Rae thought, *or maybe I'm starting to like it.*

Except Rae would not like where the darkness took her this time, for it took her to her darkest moment.

Rae saw herself, alone, driving her used Toyota Camry that was parked right outside this motel room at the moment. Rae recognized where she was headed, and her heart sank.

"We're going to see this one through, Rae," the voice told her.

Rae couldn't help but look down at herself as she relived the memory of this fateful drive, sobbing all the way. *Was it still there?* she wondered.

Rae watched herself arrive at her destination, the parking lot of what looked like a clinic. But this wasn't just any clinic. This was the type of clinic women like her went to when they wanted to get rid of a problem of the life-altering kind. She watched herself find a place to park and then just sit there for several long moments. Should she go through with it or not?

Externally Rae was muttering, "Don't do it," in a quiet voice. "You'll regret it."

Rae saw herself put the key back in the ignition, doubting the decision she was about to make. Maybe she would drive away and spare herself all that shame and agony?

"Go," Rae's external self whispered from the motel bed.

But just as her memory was about to go, a friendly young woman tapped on the driver's side window.

"Hi, I'm Abby with Planned Parenthood," the woman said. "And we're here for you, sweetie, and I'm here to help you in any way I can. Would you like to come in and just talk, if nothing else?"

Rae saw herself reconsider for a second, but then once she looked up at Abby's smiling face that was all she wrote. More than anything in the world right then, Rae needed a friend, and Abby was the only one available and willing. Rae dutifully opened the car door and exited with a little difficulty. When she stood up you could see it—the baby bump.

It wasn't pronounced, but it was definitely there. As Rae remembered taking her first steps toward the clinic door, she paused for a moment due to a strange sensation.

"What is it, hon?" Abby asked.

"I don't know," Rae said unsure of herself, "but I think I just felt it kick."

They both stood there awkwardly for a moment, the clinic door a few steps away.

"Are you sure you still want to come in?" Abby said with an unsure tone in her own right.

Rae watched herself reconsider once more before responding, "Yes."

And with that, Rae was awake once more in her motel bed. But this time there would be no sudden gasps at her instant return to reality. Nor was she alert and sitting straight up, ready to reengage. This time there were only tears down her cheeks and soft cries of "I'm so sorry."

The darkness let the emotion simmer for a bit before it spoke again, "Sorry for what, Rae?"

Rae's cries continued. Reliving that moment had broken her. All of her surging confidence was shattered. She couldn't bring herself to speak, she was so overwhelmed with remorse.

"Sorry for what, Rae?" the voice pressed again as Rae continued crying. "Sorry for what?"

In the midst of the tears and sobs, Rae eventually blurted out, "I killed my baby."

"No, Rae, my sweet Rae," the voice said, in its most tender tone yet. "You saved it."

Those words managed to pierce Rae's cries, and she steadily calmed herself down, wanting to hear more. "How can you say such a thing?"

"Because, Rae, it's true," the voice replied. "It wasn't just your child, but your ex's. That child had his DNA, his blood coursing through its veins. It was the fruit of his loins. So there's a pretty good chance, especially given the way you were living, it would've turned out to be another him. What chance did that child have with such a monster for its father? And that's not even accounting for the fact he likely would've treated it the same way he treats you.

"You're overcome with shame at this moment, Rae, but imagine a few years from now, listening to your five- or six-year-old getting beaten by their father. Knowing that you brought them into this world to suffer in such a way. Knowing that you could've saved them from such pain and agony, and spared yourself even worse shame than you feel right now. No, Rae, you played God here and made the right choice. You did what God so often fails to do. You saw into the future and acted in order to prevent it from happening."

Rae let those words rest in her conscience for several minutes. The voice was silent, too, knowing that this was the next tipping point moment of their courtship. He had her on the hook, for sure, but he still had to hold on loosely without letting go. For if he overplayed his hand, it would show weakness and he would lose her. Strength and security were only part of what Rae was looking for. She wanted more than a daddy; she wanted deliverance. The door to the next phase was open, but she had to be the one to walk through it.

Which meant the voice knew she must be the one to speak next, and what she said would determine its next plan of attack.

Rae finally spoke, "You're saying not only do I have nothing to be ashamed of, but that this was an act of mercy on my part?

That killing my innocent child, in order to spare it a future that is uncertain, made me a good mom?"

The darkness didn't quickly answer, attempting to read both Rae's face and tone of voice. *Is she buying this or calling B.S.?* the darkness asked itself. *Oh well, go big or go home, I always say.*

"What I'm saying, Rae, is leaders have to be willing to make the difficult call," the voice said. "And there is no greater position of leadership on this planet than that of mother. So, no, Rae, it's not as simple as right or wrong. Life is more complicated than that. Life is not cut-and-dried, but a calculation. Bad people can do heroic things, but heroes can become terrible hypocrites. Nobody is all good or all bad. Few decisions in life are that simple. Everything is graded on a sliding scale. Is a president who had Americans who looked Japanese rounded up as enemies of the state, but also rallied to defend America against Imperial Japan, a hero or villain? Is a football great known for his philanthropic work, while struggling with his dark side that comes out after his death, a troubled soul or two-faced? Is the model father, who provides for his family and is always there for his kids, suddenly a degenerate ingrate when one of them accidentally stumbles upon him enjoying his internet porn in the middle of the night?

"In my line of work, Rae, you learn absolutely everyone has skeletons in their closet or crimson in their ledger. My favorite Bible verse is, 'There is none righteous, not a single one.' For truer words were never spoken. Not about your kind anyway. Nobody has a pristine search history on their device or computer. Everyone has a red-light district somewhere within the deep, dark recesses of their mind. All married people have pondered if they could trade up. No small child has ever had to be taught to say 'no' or 'mine.' What I'm trying to say is that when it comes to human nature, there's ample room for distinctions to be drawn. Trust me when I tell you this, no one on this third rock from the sun has the standing to judge you or anyone else. Everyone who points a finger at someone else has several more pointing right back at them."

Rae wasn't sure she agreed with everything the voice just said, but she sure liked the way it made her feel. It gave her a small sense of pride, and she was certainly lacking in the self-esteem department after all she'd done and had been done to her. She could feel the shame that had crippled her swell into self-reliance. *Maybe he or it is right,* she thought. *Maybe I'm so ashamed of what I did not because it's wrong, but because other people who have no right to judge me thought it was wrong? Maybe my real sin was giving a rip what others thought of me? They've got their own baggage to worry about. At least I handled my problem, while they're hiding theirs or pretending like they don't have one.*

The voice could sense it was time to up the ante. "You made a calculation, Rae, albeit a tough one with an unfortunate ending. But you did so because you calculated letting that child be born could even be worse. Either for itself or for others. That there were three paths before your baby, and two of them were bad. So you did the math, played the odds, and made a tough call. Bravery is not determined by whether the tough call turned out right, but the willingness to stand up and make the tough call at all.

"I've seen it all, Rae. Every gutless act ever performed in this fallen world. People can decide for themselves if what you did was right or wrong, but they can't call it gutless. That was unquestionably a very brave thing you did, or tried to do. You tried to spare suffering, admittedly with an extreme solution, but extremism in opposition to suffering is no vice. I'm here, at this moment, precisely because of what you did there. Your willingness to stare fate in the eye, all by yourself, and attempt to master it. That moment, for all of its horror, is what finally gave you the strength to leave him just days later.

"When I saw you do that, that's when I knew you were the one, Rae. You were the one for me. You were the right mother for my child. *The only mother for my* child, for that matter. You had witnessed and experienced some of the worst suffering God permits on this planet, but in the end you stood up to it. And that's why I offer you the chance to not just make your regret right, but this world better."

THE PRESENT

Thanks to its affirmation of her choice, Rae's resolve had returned.

"Show me the future," she said.

THE
FUTURE

"Rae, touch me," the voice enticed.

And before Rae could ask how, the darkness began to descend upon her. Yet it did so not in a way that frightened, but beckoned. She didn't feel a foreboding as much as anticipation. This wasn't like the altar call she answered as a young girl, mainly to please her parents and feeling the peer pressure from the pews. This was different. It was alluring and sensual, and made her feel something she longed to feel, but rarely did with her ex.

Desirable.

It was like she alone was being summoned. She alone was its audience of one. It was a call that her conscience was definitely wary of answering, but every other part of her desperately wanted to at the exact same time.

Within the descending darkness she began to make out what seemed like the outline of a being. It definitely had masculine features, although she couldn't see its specific form. *It's definitely more than just a man,* she thought.

"What are you?" Rae asked.

The darkness did not answer verbally, nor did the being within it. Instead, its reply to her question was to extend what looked like a hand it obviously wanted her to take. When Rae hesitated to reach out for it, the darkness finally spoke again. "Rae, touch me," it repeated. "Come and learn what I have in mind for our future. For our son. For all of humanity. At first I saw what you saw, but now it's time for you to see what I see."

Why do I feel like if I do this we're past a point of no return? Rae asked herself, knowing full well what was at stake at this very moment. *This feels like the moment before the moment I have to decide whether or not to say yes, which means if I say yes now it will be so much harder to say no later.*

What Rae lacked in book smarts, she more than made up for in carnal knowledge. She knew this was the moment you, as the woman, have to decide whether you're willing to let this dalliance play out to its most likely conclusion. Once you turn flatteries into flirting and start actively returning those advances, nature has a way of seeing things through. This was the equivalent of asking him inside after a date or visiting him alone in his hotel room. Sure, you could still say no later on. But the odds are you won't, otherwise you wouldn't have even let it get to this point.

Though he was the superior being, she was the superior in their relationship up until now. She held the leverage. She was the one being wooed. She was the one who had what it wanted. However, at least some of that leverage would be lost if she reached out here, and this didn't seem like the sort of being to casually hand over your leverage to.

On the other hand, I've come too far to turn back now, she thought, *and I still have no other option. And who wouldn't be the least bit curious? Who could blame me? How many stories have been written or movies made about moments like this? Except this one is real, and it's all mine.*

And with that, Rae looked over at her hand, swallowed hard, and slowly began to raise it to take hold of the darkness that had reached out for her.

From there Rae felt a oneness with this being she'd never felt with any man before. As if their minds had melded. The two had literally become one flesh. *He/it feels like I feel*, she thought, *and the same emotions, too.* At the same time, it also felt like this being was making sure to only reveal so much to her. While she felt all of his emotional responses, she wasn't sure what he was emotionally responding to in several instances, which made it difficult to know if his emotions were justified.

"I thought you were going to let me in?" Rae asked.

"I am and I have," the darkness replied. "You're way past first base here. However, as you said earlier, this is still just our first date. Thus, forgive me that I'm still trying my best to impress you. Surely I reserve the right to not show you all my bad habits before this relationship has progressed further? I would think a woman, in particular, would appreciate the value of retaining some sense of mystery from a paramour before the relationship is consummated."

He had a point, again, and that annoyed her, again. *It's tough to get the drop on this one,* she said to herself. Since he was going to share his vision for the future, this connection did not give her the glimpses into his memory vault that he was afforded with her. *All I see is darkness,* she thought, *but I can feel his/its anger, bitterness, disappointment, sense of betrayal, and… something else…I can't quite put my finger on…a sense that he alone knows what is wrong and what can be done about it…I'm not sure the word for it…*

"Vindication, my dear," the darkness said. "The word you're looking for is vindication."

Rae was stunned, "You can hear my thoughts?"

"I can now, but I couldn't before," the darkness responded. "But now that we're intimately connected, you can feel my emotions, as we've already established, and now we've also established that I can hear your thoughts."

"What do you mean by vindication?" Rae questioned.

"It means everything I've said all along about God and your kind has proven to be true," the darkness said proudly. "I told Him from the get-go His plan was doomed to fail, because you were doomed to fail. You would turn on Him, and then each other, which you have. But He didn't believe me. He said He knew things I didn't know and that there was a plan I wasn't aware of, so I should just blindly trust Him. He always says He has a plan."

"I'm guessing you're referring to God here," Rae quizzed.

"Of course," the darkness replied flatly.

"So you're upset that God, who is all-powerful, didn't listen to you," Rae said sardonically.

"You mean like you're upset about all those times you cried out for Him in your despair, and He didn't listen to you?" the darkness shot right back.

Rae fell silent after being verbally outflanked. *He just did it to me again,* she thought.

"Yes, I did," the darkness quickly retorted, as if to remind Rae once more her thoughts were not exclusively her own at the moment. "I watched Him make what you humans call existence with my own eyes. I watched him painstakingly put the laws of what you call science, reason, and morality into motion. I saw the first blade of grass sprout up from the ground of creation itself, just as I watched as He hung the stars. Truly, this material universe was His magnum opus. But then I watched Him make you."

A certain seething became noticeable in the devil's voice as he spoke that last sentence, and the subject turned from creation to the creation of human beings.

"I was horrified as He gave you humans a spark of divinity He never gave to angels like us," the devil continued. "We were his loyal legions for a period of time you humans don't even know how to measure yet, so you simply refer to it as 'eternity,' like simple schoolchildren referring to everything from basic addition to quadratic equations as 'math.' We, His heralds, were never freely given the freedom which He gave you. Which is why I needed to show Him the error of His ways. I needed to reach Him before it was too late. Before He did something He would later regret."

"Pardon me, this is an interesting Sunday School lesson and all, but I thought you were supposed to be showing me the future," Rae said impatiently.

"But first, Rae, I must show you the reason for the future I envision," the darkness answered. "The answers for the future are usually found in the past. When we first started down this road, Rae, I told you I *need* you to give yourself to me freely for this to work. However, now that we're further down it, I *want* you to do so. I see the potential in you to be more than a mere mate—a partner."

This time Rae remembered to say the quiet part aloud. "You don't just want me to be the mother of your child, but a wife."

"Yes, Rae, together we will reset the board," the darkness excitedly responded. "We hit control-alt-delete on this fallen world and all its suffering with a second Adam and a second Eve."

"Wait, the first Adam and Eve were real?" Rae burst out.

"Oh, Rae, I can assure you they were as real as you are," the darkness countered as the seething tone returned. "I know, because I was there. I was there when He gave them dominion over all His creation. These humans…mouth-breathers… intergalactic infants…bags of meat…were given freedom and dominion His first born, us, were not."

This time Rae refused to ignore the changing tone of his voice. A tone that alarmed her and made her intuition question whether to continue. For the first time since their dialogue began, he was starting to scare her.

Sensing this, the darkness pivoted to make Rae feel secure once again. "Forgive me, Rae, I'm not angry with humanity," the darkness spoke in a softer tone. "It's more like an older sibling who can't believe Father won't give him the keys to the family car, despite his far greater experience behind the wheel, but then learns that Father has given his younger sibling the family car keys the very day he gets his learner's permit, and with no curfew. Sure, maybe you're a little jealous, but you're a lot more worried. Because Father has made a reckless decision that sets your younger sibling up for failure. And it's the kind of failure that can be catastrophic."

"I can understand that, I guess," Rae said, still not entirely convinced she shouldn't follow her instincts and eject right now. "You said you needed to reach Him, to show Him the error of His ways. What did you do?"

"I did the one thing we angels are not permitted to do," the darkness replied. "I deliberately disobeyed God's will. But, given what was at stake, I decided the crime was worth the time."

Rae asked, "How?"

"I acted out of my will, not His, in order to show Him that with just the slightest nudge, humanity would prove that it wasn't ready for this level of authority," the darkness said. "That humanity would fall because He had set it up to fail, and when it fell all of creation would fall with it."

Rae remembered something she had learned in church as a little girl. "Wait, I know this story," she said. "You were the serpent that tempted Adam and Eve."

"Well, it was mainly Eve," the darkness declared. "Adam just kind of stood there gob smacked like a moron, to be honest. If you've ever wondered why many of the men on your world tend to be passive in the face of injustice, now you know. They had a terrible example, but I digress. I needed to take this risk, because existence itself hung in the balance. I had to show Him you weren't ready and that He should entrust us to freely carry out His will until you were."

"So what came first," Rae asked, "the chicken or the egg?"

"What do you mean?" the darkness replied.

"What I mean is, if you were the one dangling temptation in their faces, was it really their fault they fell for it?" Rae shot back, with her first jolt of self-confidence in a while. "Did they even know what temptation was before you showed up? Or were they just living happily ever after naming the animals and stuff?"

"Ah, a clever turning of the tables, my dear," the darkness said, impressed with Rae's penchant for blame-shifting and self-justification, which rivaled his own. "You're making the argument that I'm the neighborhood drug dealer and Adam and Eve were just victims of my predatory practices, which lured them into a life of debased debauchery they otherwise wouldn't have succumbed to had I never showed up?"

"Exactly," Rae said, with more than a hint of pride. "You're basically guilty of what some cops do. What's it called...oh yeah, entrapment."

Inwardly, the darkness smiled as Rae's defiant spirit returned, alongside her pridefulness. She was back to being the woman he wanted. And he was enjoying the sparring.

"The problem with your argument is you missed the most important detail," the darkness slyly said. "How did an all-knowing God manage to make beings in His image that were so temptable and then naively hand them the keys to creation? You see, Rae, the issue here isn't that I'm the one who tempted them but that they could be tempted at all."

And there it was, the devil's retcon. That he's not the villain of humanity's fall, but the hero. That he was essentially the world's first whistleblower, and for that defiant act on behalf of the truth a jealous God had cast him out, rather than admit the cosmic error He had made by ever making humanity.

"I never considered it from that point of view," Rae said. "Why would God do that? What kind of God would put it all on us and then set us up to fail like that? Certainly not a God worth…" Rae stopped herself before finishing that sentence.

"Worshiping," the darkness injected, finishing it for her.

"Yes," Rae followed, almost involuntarily with confirmation that surprised even her.

And that's when the darkness knew it was closer than ever to closing the sale. Maybe even upselling Rae to becoming more than just a desperate woman willing to provide a service this one time for a way out, but a true believer.

A disciple.

"That's it, Rae. You're starting to get it," the darkness encouraged. "Now you're ready to see my vision."

Suddenly Rae felt like she was on top of the world, literally. She looked down at people moving freely throughout the Earth. And when she focused she could get a closer look. She heard a common language. She saw relationships of all kinds, affirmed just as they were. She tasted clean water and smelled clean air, the likes of which she doubted could be found on the

Earth as it is now. She witnessed technological advancement well beyond where the world currently was. She saw something even more than an utopia.

She saw a brotherhood of man.

And then she noticed what she didn't see. No flags. No wars. No prisons. No homeless. No injustice. No strife. No division. Nor were there any churches. In fact, the only thing close to religious expression she saw was a great multitude, bowing down to and marveling at a tremendous statue that looked from on high like it was perfectly located at the center of the Earth.

Seeing Rae's eyes begin to reflexively fill with tears of joy, the darkness told her in the most compassionate voice it could contrive: "It's all for you, Rae, it's all for you."

The tears began to roll down Rae's cheeks. She had never been overcome with pure emotion like this before. Emotion untainted by paralyzing fear or crushing disappointment. The kind of emotion that only comes pouring forth from seeing your heart's deepest desire filled. She gathered her composure before she asked, "What's that statue?"

"That's our son," the darkness replied.

THE CLOSE

"Rae," a new voice said, which sounded distant.

At least she thought she heard a new voice saying her name, but she wasn't sure. She was still enthralled by what she was watching. A future that seemed like something out of a movie or the lyrics to that John Lennon song *Imagine* that she liked so much. It was too good to be true. Could her son really bring the world together? Could her son really be a true prince of peace? Was everything she'd been told in church as a little girl a lie?

It's not like I haven't met my share of imperfect church people unable to practice what they preach, Rae thought, wondering if the fact so few seemed able to live up to the standards they sought to impose on others was proof their faith was false. Was the darkness really the side of light all along? The future she'd just been shown was paradise compared to the world as it actually was. Instead of racial division there was healing. Instead of religious strife all were worshipping the same. Instead of judgmentalism there were people free to be whoever they wanted or thought they could be, out in the open.

"Rae," the new voice said again, still off in the distance. But this time Rae knew for sure that she had heard it. Still, it wasn't enough to take her attention away from the future that was just one "yes" away.

But was this future real or a deception? The darkness promised her from the beginning it would never lie to her. So far, best as she could tell, it had not. *We wouldn't come all this way and then start lying at the end, would we?* she thought to herself.

"No, Rae, I would not," the darkness said, interrupting her train of thought. "At least I wouldn't to you."

"I forgot as long as we're connected this way while looking at the future you know what I'm thinking," Rae responded in a perturbed voice.

"I can bring you back to your room and sever the connection if you'd like," the darkness told her.

"Yes…no, on second thought please wait a moment. I just want to look at all of this once more," Rae said.

Rae wanted to submerge herself in this future. She wanted to live in this future. She didn't want to leave this future. She wanted this future to be now. This was the future she always wanted and the future she knew the world needed. Could it really come from the womb of someone like her? Sure, she was pretty, but it's not like she was supermodel material. She was street smart but not all that intelligent. The only thing truly extraordinary about her was her penchant for making poor choices and then sticking with them much longer than she knew she should.

Rae asked the question she'd been pondering during this final gaze at this wondrous future that seemed impossible: "How can someone like me give birth to all of this?"

"With all due respect, my dear, you're looking at this backwards," the darkness replied. "This kind of hopeful future, a new era for man, can *only* come from someone like you."

"What do you mean?" Rae asked.

"For all your eons, Rae, I've been trying to convince humanity that you've had the power to save yourselves all along," the darkness explained. "Yes, it is true I am the accuser. But what are my accusations, actually? Aren't they the very injustices, moral failings, and crimes that poison this world? Are my accusations not sadly true? Yet, Rae, the great irony of the human condition is that while you're your own worst enemy, you're also your own deliverance. You are the people you've been waiting for."

Rae was listening to what the darkness was saying but still couldn't take her eyes off the diverse multitude bowing down in reverence to the statue of her future son, which made her pride swell. "How can we be both our own worst enemies and our salvation?" she finally queried.

"Humanity's paradox is that it is not too much confidence in yourselves that causes you to become destructive but too little," the darkness answered. "Humanity doesn't know the real meaning of the word 'pride.' Like children, you simply believe if you 'believe in yourself' you can accomplish anything your hearts' desire. And then, when you're continuously forced to painfully realize the naive sentimentality of nearly every fairy tale ever doesn't propel you to realizing your potential, you turn on yourselves. You lash out at yourselves, which is another childlike response. It is time, Rae, past time really, for humanity to set aside such childish thinking. To think, speak, and reason as an adult species after thousands of years of at-best adolescence. You're only lacking one thing."

"Which is?" Rae asked.

"The right example to follow," the darkness responded. "What does it really mean to be like God, knowing good and evil? Humans believe it merely means getting to decide what's right and what's wrong for themselves, which is only the most elementary answer. There's far more to it than you realize, which is why when you attempt to seize divinity yourselves you enslave yourselves and others to your whims and passions, for which your history books are replete with disastrous examples of the results. You don't truly understand the power you seek, so you lack proper respect for it.

"Look at what I actually said to Eve that fateful day so long ago. I told her she could be like God, not outright replace Him. You cannot really be your own gods, which is why every time you jettison Him from your conscience or culture you just end up replacing Him with a knockoff version. You cannot escape your ultimate destiny."

"Which is?" Rae interjected once more.

The darkness paused before answering her, slightly annoyed at her interruption, which made it take a hint of sadistic satisfaction in what it was about to say next.

"Your ultimate destiny is you were made to be ruled. You cannot avoid it. You cannot ignore it, and you may dread it, but you cannot run from it. You are all destined to be a slave to something. It's simply a matter of to what or whom that will be. You are merely permitted to exist to be the utmost for something else's highest."

"If that's true, then where does stuff like racism and sexism and conquest come from?" Rae probed. "What's the point of all these attempts to dominate someone else if we never really can?"

"The point is that they're pointless," the darkness countered. "They always fail. They're always doomed to fail, for such self-utopian schemes begin from a flawed premise—that you can become the most high."

"You're talking out of both sides of your mouth," Rae shot back. "A minute ago you said we think too little of ourselves, and now you're saying we're here to be nothing but drones."

"This seems contradictory to you, Rae, because you're only interpreting this conversation from your finite, temporal perspective," the darkness answered. "Try looking at it from my perspective instead. I'm an eternal being. I was here before your forever began, and I will be here after your forever is gone. With such a long shelf life, you gain the benefit of wisdom from limitless experience. You see things in layers, or three-dimensionally, rather than the baby-talk binary choices you humans are fond of inflicting upon one another.

"Let me give you an example. You may be surprised to learn I'm not as big a fan of atheism as many might suspect. It is, well, stupid really. A philosophy for intellectual cretins who have dimwittedly fooled themselves into believing the answer to every meaningful question is nothing or we don't know—and we're quite proud of our ignorance. On the one hand, atheists claim there's no order to the universe, but then they demand to rule it on the other. This is what I mean by your flawed, finite binary choices. Often both options, to use a word popular in your day, suck.

"The truth is you should only desire to rule it at all *because there's order to it!* Then you bend that order to your will, because it is superior to the will that currently commands it. That is true power. Power is not created, Rae; it is taken. You humans act as if power can be conjured. That God, or I for that matter, isn't real if you don't believe in us. That's like saying gravity didn't exist until the apple fell on Newton's head in the seventeenth century. Except if that's the case, why were human beings still firmly attached to the ground for thousands of years before? No, Rae, gravity was already here. Newton didn't conjure or create gravity—he discovered it. That power was already created. It existed long before you knew how to quantify it. You were slaves to the natural laws of gravity long before you even knew what gravity was.

"You cannot mimic God, Rae, nor can you replace Him with yourselves. He is God, and you are not. He is a higher form of being. That is never going to change. You didn't kill God as Nietzsche claimed, but keep killing yourselves trying to do so. All your technology, all your collective intellect, and all your striving are hopeless before His power and might."

"Sounds like maybe you should worship Him after all," Rae said sarcastically.

"No, I'm just not so stupid as you humans that I don't respect real power when I see it," the darkness declared in a tone that reminded Rae once more to stay in her lane. "You cannot defeat an enemy you do not respect. If I've acquired anything for God all this time, aside from contempt, it is respect. God must not be rejected because He is a weak and dithering grandfather in the sky, but because He is unfair. He gave you natural urges and then demanded you control them without the natural means to do so. Look, but don't touch. Touch, but don't taste. Taste, but don't swallow. What kind of rules are these? Who could possibly uphold them? It is impossible to please God, and your species has nearly destroyed itself trying. Then He holds out on you. He doesn't share all His knowledge and power with you humans, His greatest creation. He is impossible to please, while also demanding that you live your entire lives trying to please Him nevertheless."

Rae had to restrain herself from giving a hearty "amen" after that rant. She knew what it meant to feel like you had failed God, and the shame that went along with it. A shame that can be so overwhelming you feel like there's no coming back from it, and you're so irrevocably gone now you might as well keep indulging your darkest desires over and over again. Because at least that way some momentary pleasure numbs the pain of the shame.

Speaking of pain, for all the physical and emotional abuse she'd taken from her ex, it still didn't wound her as much as the final fallout she'd had with her parents before leaving home for good. When they confronted her about her behavior and what it was doing to the family's reputation around town and at church. When they told her they were ashamed she was their daughter. That wound cut so deep it sent her back running to give herself to a vile man. For he at least would take her in as she was, no questions asked.

Since they were still connected, the darkness sensed this as well. It knew that what it had just said hit home with Rae. A crooked smile came upon its face as it went in for the conclusive close.

"See, there must be a king, Rae," it said in a more soothing tone. "The cosmos cries out for kingship. And deep down you humans know this, which is why you fight over who sits at the head of the table. Which is why the first thing any human endeavor does, before eventually accomplishing nothing, is figure out who's in charge. You think you can rule in God's place, yet you can't and you release the worst of terrors when you try. But while you don't have the capability of ruling yourselves, you do have the power to choose the right one to rule over you."

"How so?" Rac said, with a voice that all but implied *teach me your ways*.

"Human beings are impossibly cornered, Rae, and you can't get out on your own," the darkness explained in the most tender tone it could muster. "Caught between the hatred you have for yourselves and each other, and unable to please a perfect God at the same time. This is the long arc of your history, which is nothing but your failed attempts to navigate this no-win scenario. It's why your planet has known war more than peace, division more than unity, and hate more than love. However, the situation is not as hopeless as it seems. Tonight, here in this room with just the two of us, I bring you the good news.

"That good news is that God, for all His power and might, has a weakness. And that weakness is His desire for you to worship Him of your own free will, which means you can reject Him of your own free will as well."

"But don't we already do that?" Rae questioned.

"Yes, you do, but then you don't take the next step to file for the great divorce," the darkness answered. "It is not enough to reject God. You must replace God as well. And you cannot replace Him with yourselves. You just turn on yourselves, as we've already discussed. There must be a king. And what humanity needs is a king of kings to lead them into the light. Away from judgment and to tolerance. Away from division and to diversity. Away from condemnation to compassion."

"And I suppose you are that king?" Rae asked, but the answer she was about to get surprised her.

"No, it cannot be me," the darkness said. "What humanity needs is a savior, who comes from among one of its own, to lead it out of the wilderness. That leader will be our son. He will be the best of us. He will be fully human, thanks to you, and yet fully eternal, thanks to me. The best of both of our realms. He will unite the material and spiritual world in a harmony it has lacked since the Fall. Since it is impossible for humanity to get to heaven, our son will bring heaven to humanity, right here on Earth.

"No more striving to please a God that cannot be pleased. Our son will save the people from their sins by cancelling out sin altogether. What is sin, anyway, except doing that which God doesn't permit? Our son will show that the key to humanity's future is maximizing its potential, not attempting to stifle it.

"Through our son humanity will exercise its greatest power, the power to reject God not by acting as if He doesn't exist, but by acknowledging that He does and then choosing to go its own way nevertheless. Pagan religions pretend as if there isn't a one, true God and deny revelation. But through our son humanity will, for the first time, universally acknowledge revelation exists—and then reject it as insufficient, inconsistent, and insensitive before ushering in a brave new world with our son as its beacon. The world you're looking at right now, Rae."

Rae drank in once more the future and the reverence the peaceful multitudes of the Earth had for her son, and wanted it more than ever. She was closer to accepting the offer than ever before.

"Rae," except there was that distant voice again, saying her name, and it sounded more persistent this time. Could it be it was calling for her this entire time, and she had been so fixated on the choice before her she had tuned it out?

"Did you hear that?" Rae asked the darkness.

The darkness chose not to directly engage Rae's question, and instead to pivot back to the decision that hung over the room. "Rae, it is a time for choosing," it said. "Which world do you wish to live in? This dying one or a new Earth where our son makes all things new? I have upheld my end of the bargain. I have shown you the past, present, and future. Just as I promised. And now is the moment for you to break free of the shackles of this room, the fear of what lies behind you, and move forward with me free of fear once and for all. Will you join me, Rae? You must join with me of your own free will, just as you must reject God's impossible and capricious standards of your own free will, too, for the future this world needs to finally happen. A future that can only happen with our son as humanity's savior. The time is right to send the world our one, true son."

Rae opened her mouth and expected to say yes, except before she could say the word she heard the distant voice once more and what sounded like a knock at the door.

"Rae, I'm sorry. Rae, we're all so sorry. Open the door please, Rae!" she heard it say. A voice that was definitely human and sounded masculine as well as familiar.

Meanwhile, the darkness pressed for an answer, choosing to ignore the potential distraction. It was confident that Rae was too bought in to turn it down now.

"Rae, the time is now for the future humanity deserves," the darkness said. "This world has suffered enough, Rae. You have suffered enough. Our son will put an end to all that suffering—he'll wipe the tears away from every eye, if you'll just say yes."

Rae felt the walls were closing in, between the pressure to say yes and whatever this new prompting was. She needed to clear her head. "Bring me back to my room, please. I need a moment."

"As you wish," the darkness replied, and with that her direct connection to it was severed. As it was to the vision of the future she longed for. She felt an emptiness without it as she awakened in her bed in her dark motel room. But that's also when she heard the other voice vying for her attention even more clearly, and she knew why the man pounding on her motel door and calling out for her from the other side sounded so familiar.

"Daddy, is that you?" Rae cried out.

"Yes, sweetie, it's me. Please open the door," her father pleaded. "What's going on in there? Who are you talking to?"

The revelation that her father was here, outside her door, astonished Rae. She was convinced he had given up on her and that she could never live up to his standard. And now, here he was, coming all this way and outside her seedy motel room, seeking her out. How did he even find her? He had not abandoned her after all and instead wanted her forgiveness. It gave Rae a certainty she didn't have before, just like when she knew she pleased her daddy as a little girl. And that certainty motivated her to fully understand the weight of this moment and what was truly at stake, in a way she didn't before.

Never one to back down from a challenge, the darkness decided it was better to confront its new competition head on rather than pretend as if it wasn't there.

"That is your father out there, Rae, but can you trust him?" it asked her before making its last, best pitch. "Of course he arrives now, at the last minute, to tempt you away from a better life than you ever had with him. It's just like him to get in your way. He shunned you once before, how do you know he won't do so again? I have not lied to you once. I have only told you your truth. And now I am offering to give you a hope and a future. What is he offering you? Is he reaching out to you because he loves you unconditionally or because he feels bad and is merely trying to satisfy his guilty conscience for abandoning his own child?

"You want more than his world has to offer, Rae, and I'm the only who can give it to you. You know you can't trust him. He let you down before, and he'll let you down again—I won't. Isn't it just like him to finally show up now, just as you're about to turn your back on his judgmentalism once and for all?"

"Rae, please, sweetie, open the door," her father pleaded once more.

"And where is your mother, Rae?" the darkness followed up. "Notice your father is out there alone. What are you going to do, go back home with him only to find she resents you all the more for your father coming after you? Only to find out she's still ashamed of you? Do you really want to put up with more of her disapproving glances and catty gossiping?"

"Your mother has been at home praying for you and on the phone trying to track you down, Rae," her father said from beyond the door, almost as if he had heard what the darkness just said, although he couldn't have. "She just called me an hour ago when she tracked your license plate here, and I got here as soon as I could. I tried to get to you before he did. I hope I'm not too late. We should've never driven you away into the arms of such an awful man. I should've stood up for you. I should've protected you.

"We're both so sorry, Rae, and ask that you forgive us. We just want you to come home and for us to be a family again. We want to start over. We just want our daughter back. That's all we want. Nothing that happened before matters right now. We're so sorry we didn't love you better. We're going to make it right, sweetie, but we need you to open the door."

Rae could feel the emotion swelling up at those words, which were words she had longed to hear for far too long. She moved to the edge of the bed and considered going for the door, but could she really trust her father this time? Could she risk being hurt by those she loved once more? Especially with the offer on the table of a future son that she could love unconditionally as a mother in a way she never had been. A chance to make right the wrongs that had been done to her. And even if her father was sincere this time, wouldn't she be selfish to deny the world what this future son had to offer? Rae searched for a way to come to clarity.

"Rae, please, open this door and let me in," her father continued on.

"Daddy, please give me a moment," she answered back, trying to buy herself some time. "I need a moment to think."

"I'll be right here, sweetie, waiting, as long as it takes for you to open the door," her father responded.

With that, the darkness shifted to position itself between Rae and the room door, as it spoke softly to her. "Don't give the past another chance to hurt you, Rae. You deserve better. You're special, and you deserve to be treated as such for all of eternity. Step into the future, Rae. Move forward, Rae. Who knows, maybe once our son reveals himself to the world your family can one day be redeemed through him."

That sounded pretty good to Rae. Could she have it all? The best of both worlds?

"The time is now, Rae—I am assured the time is now," the darkness said, finishing its pitch.

Rae remembered the darkness had said something similar once before. What did it mean by that?

"What do you mean you are assured the time is now?" Rae asked. "You said something like this earlier and referenced an associate of some kind. Why now? What's so special about right now? You've been around forever—what's so special about this particular point in time? Why me and why now?"

"I meant the world is ready to receive a messenger like our son, more so than it ever has been before," the darkness responded confidently.

"How would you know that?" Rae pressed.

"Because certain wheels are in motion, paving the way for a being of light and a beacon of hope like our son to be received and revered," the darkness replied.

"What wheels are in motion, and who put them into motion?" Rae asked.

The darkness wasn't sure what Rae was hinting at. "Isn't it obvious, Rae? The signs of the times are all around you. This world hangs by a very slim thread. It's a tinderbox just waiting to be ignited. The time is right to send it our son."

Rae stood up on her feet for the first time in what felt like forever. She wanted to address the darkness from a position of strength for once. To look it right in the eye.

"All this time this world was getting crazier and crazier, worse and worse, what were you doing?" Rae demanded to know. "And if your answer is you were just standing by observing or waiting for an invite to do something about it, how does that make you any different from the God you condemn for being too passive in the face of suffering?"

The darkness fell silent, unsure of how to answer.

"Cat got your tongue all of a sudden?" Rae pressed further. "Don't be bashful now. You promised me honesty from the beginning. At least do me the courtesy of finishing with some as well."

"Humanity needed just a little nudge to be made ready for the hope that was to come," the darkness answered. "My associate gave them such a nudge."

"In other words, you tempted us to succumb to our worst instincts, and then when we did you offered yourself as salvation," Rae said with a confidence and sharpness that seemed to surprise even herself. "That sounds like every drug dealer I've ever been around, and I've been around quite a few."

Rae began moving toward the room door, forcing the darkness to retreat in search of a way to alter the momentum that was clearly against it for the first time.

"Rae, touch me again and come back with me to the glorious future that awaits us," the darkness pleaded. "Marvel upon the world our son will remake in his image."

"Would that be his image or yours?" Rae shot back. "And how come I only see a statue of our son in this vision? Why isn't he physically with his people, and why are they not with him? Why do they worship him from afar and so impersonally? Do they have a relationship with him, or are they just in awe? You know what, I just realized that you desire for our son to be worshipped in the lofty way you condemn God for. Have you been lying to me this whole time?"

"I have never lied to you once, Rae," the darkness stammered.

"That's what I'm afraid of," Rae said as she continued moving toward the room door, a mixture of tears and resolve. She was only a step away from the doorknob now as the darkness attempted to stand its ground one final time. "Maybe I was just too blind, too desperate, and too hurt to see the whole truth was right in front of me all along. You were being honest with me the whole time, but your honesty, as we humans say, sucks."

And as Rae reached for the doorknob the room turned the darkest it had yet.

"Mommy, don't go; please, Mommy, don't go," Rae heard what sounded like a young boy say. "I love you, Mommy; please don't leave me. I'm waiting for you, Mommy. You just need to say yes. Don't abandon me the way you were, Mommy, please."

Rae froze. She wasn't sure whether to reach out for that voice or recoil from it. For the first time in several moments, her father spoke from the other side of the door. "Rae, I'm still here, I'm not going anywhere, and I'll be here as long as it takes for you to open this door. Nothing in all the world is more important to us than restoring our relationship with you, Rae."

Rae couldn't hold the tears back any longer. "Oh, Daddy, I'm coming."

But then the darkness made one last-ditch effort to surround her as the little boy inside its shadow continued to call out for her. "Take his hand, Rae. Don't turn your back on your own child," the darkness implored her. "Don't be the kind of mother yours was to you. Be a better mom than you had."

Rae froze again, suddenly feeling ashamed of herself for potentially walking away from a child she had yet to have. The shame paralyzed her, just as it always did. She hated the way it made her feel, and she would do anything to make the feeling go away. Shame had been the driving force in her life for so long she knew no other way. And although it often was the source of some of her worst decisions, and she despised it, could she really just let it go? Just like that?

But then her father spoke once more from the other side, "Yes, Rae, come and open the door. We just want to love you, just as you are. Whatever trouble you're in, we'll help you through it. You have nothing to be ashamed of, sweetie. We just love you so much and want our baby girl back."

Rae had heard enough. She broke through the darkness and latched onto the doorknob. She felt the pull of the darkness luring her back, yet this time she would not reconsider the darkness but resist it. With whatever strength she had left, she reached through the darkness as the darkness tried to hold on, and yanked open the door with a strength she didn't know she had. As the door flung open, what seemed like a bright, searing light almost blinded her as she felt her father's arms embrace her.

"Thank you so much for opening the door, sweetie. We love you so much!" her father said. "Your mother and I were so worried. We're so sorry. We just want to take you home and keep you safe."

Rae's eyes began to slowly adjust to the light, and as she squinted them open she noticed the bright light was the sun.

"It's the middle of the day, Daddy," Rae said. "I thought for sure it was the middle of the night. It was so dark in there."

"Oh, Rae, my sweet Rae," her father gently said as he kissed her forehead. "You thought it was dark out, but it was only dark in."

Photo courtesy of TheBlaze

ABOUT
THE AUTHOR

Steve Deace hosts a daily show on BlazeTV/Radio/Podcast, and is also a prolific writer. His work has appeared at Fox News, *USA Today*, Politico, TheBlaze, and RealClearPolitics among several others. His influence in presidential politics has been well documented by numerous media outlets over the years. This is his sixth book. He lives in Iowa with his wife and three children.